S0-CPB-470

My Sister Makes Me Happy!

by Evelyn Daviddi

To my daughter, Zoe
—E.D.

Milk & Cookies Press
a division of ibooks, inc.
24 West 25th Street
New York, NY 10010

Distributed by Publishers Group West

My sister makes me happy...

because she
always gives
me the best
presents.
Happy
birthday
to you!

My sister makes me happy...

when she
shares her
candy with me.

My sister makes me happy...

when she introduces me to
her friends' older brothers.

My sister told me you were cute!

My sister

makes me happy...

Try these on!

because she always knows what looks good on me.

My sister makes me happy...

when she cleans up our room before Mom sees it.

Your room looks better than ever!

My sister makes me happy...

because she
always makes
popcorn when
we watch
movies together.

My sister makes me happy...

because she always gets the soccer ball out from under the car.

My sister makes me happy...

but, at
the same
time,

My sister makes me mad...
but, at the same time,
Turn over

This outfit looks so much better on me!

My sister makes me mad...

when she steals my clothes.

My sister makes me mad...

when she forgets to tell me who called.

A boy called, but I can't remember his name...
8.00 p.m.
Have to call...
?

because she always spies on me.
I can't believe she kissed him!
I LOVE TOM
Monday
MY FIRST KISS

My sister makes me mad...

when she uses my computer.

My sister makes me mad...

when she puts
stickers on all
my things.

My sister makes me mad...

because Mom always takes her side.
Mom says we can listen to my station.

My sister makes me mad...

because
she never
has to walk
the dog.

My sister makes me mad...

My Sister Makes Me Mad!

by Evelyn Daviddi

Cover art by Evelyn Daviddi
Cover design by Edie Weinberg

My Sister Makes Me Happy! / My Sister Makes Me Mad!

A publication of Milk & Cookies Press, a division of ibooks, inc.

Distributed by Publishers Group West
1700 Fourth Street, Berkeley, CA 94710

ibooks, inc.
24 West 25th Street, 11th floor, New York, NY 10010
ISBN: 1-59687-170-9
First ibooks, inc. printing: May 2006
10 9 8 7 6 5 4 3 2 1
Editor – Dinah Dunn
Associate Editor – Robin Bader
Assistant Editor – Maureen Lo
Designed by Edie Weinberg
Library of Congress Cataloging-in-Publication Data available
Manufactured in China